"Peace is generated from consciousness, one person at a time. *Where Peace Lives* is a beautiful invitation to people of every age to engage in the pursuit of peace."
- **Deepak Chopra**, author (*Peace is the Way*)

"I was charmed."
- **Gore Vidal**, author

"When I finished *Where Peace Lives* I felt the same way I did after putting down *The Little Prince*; grateful for the magic of a fable to delight, inspire and educate, all at the same time."
- **Jane Seymour**, actress, honorary national chairperson for City Hearts

"In this book, children and adults can find inspiration and get to the source of what really matters in their own lives. It is a roadmap to the soul."
- **Arianna Huffington**, author/editor Huffington Post (*Fanatics and Fools: The Game Plan For Winning Back America*, *The Fourth Instinct*, *Picasso*)

"*Where Peace Lives* is the coolest ride. It is an adventure down a new 'rabbit hole' with pearls of wisdom on the other side."
- **Penny Marshall**, director ("Big," "A League Of Their Own," "Awakenings")

"The children of our world deserve peace. It is their right and their divine destiny. *Where Peace Lives* unlocks the keys each of us must hold to become a more conscious peacemaker."
- **Debbie Ford**, #1 *New York Times* best-selling author (*The Dark Side of the Light Chasers* and *The Best Year of Your Life*)

"Imaginative, colorful, lyrical and heartfelt, *Where Peace Lives* is an unforgettable adventure to the magical places where peace truly lives. Treat yourself to the journey. It's worth it."
- **Penney Finkelman Cox**, producer ("Terms of Endearment," "Shrek," "Honey, I Shrunk the Kids," "Antz")

"*Where Peace Lives* has a clear, resonant message that rings true for all ages. It will be read aloud and treasured in the tradition of classic, thought-provoking children's literature like the *Chronicles of Narnia*, *Charlotte's Web* and *The Little Prince*.

- **Lois Sarkisian**, founder, Every Picture Tells A Story...

"*Where Peace Lives* is an imaginative, beautiful, important story, a must-read for children and adults alike. After all, what could be more vital to our world than rediscovering the keys to peace and knowing we can make a difference? This is a classic in the making."

- **Daphne Rose Kingma**, author (*Finding True Love, Coming Apart, Future of Love*)

"It is delightful how gracefully author Debbie Robins weaves the teachings of King, Buddha, Gandhi, Christ, Moses and Muhammad into the most extraordinary wonder tale. If Lewis Carroll or Saint- Exupery were still alive, they would approve of her choices."

- **Nicholas Lore**, author/coach (*The Pathfinder*)

"The characters were cleverly done -- the names were especially humorous. Yes, it's short, but it was also one of the most interesting books of the summer! The illustrations were beautiful."

- **Rachel** and **Debra Marcus**, ages 11 and 15

"A wonderful story with a great message. It's going to be a hit."

- **Les Edgerton**, author/educator (*Finding Your Voice, Hooked: Write Fiction That Grabs The Reader at Page One and Never Lets Go*)

This book is going to change the world!

- **Wendy Newman**, M.A., founder of Person-Centered Branding® and personal branding coach to celebrities, athletes and executives

Winner of the Editor's Choice Award, San Diego State University's Annual Writers Conference - 2005

CAMBRIDGE HOUSE PRESS
New York, NY 10001
www.camhousepress.com

Library of Congress Cataloging-in-Publication Data
Robins, Debbie, 1956-
Where Peace lives / by Debbie Robins; Illustrations by
Victor Robert.
p. cm.
ISBN 978-0-9787213-7-4 (alk. paper)
1. Angels--Fiction. 2. Peace--Fiction. 3. New Age fiction.
I. Title.

PS3618.O3176W47 2007
813'.6--dc22

2007011074

10 9 8 7 6 5 4 3 2

This book was written, printed and bound in the
United States of America.

Where Peace Lives

DEBBIE ROBINS

Illustrations By
VICTOR ROBERT

CAMBRIDGE HOUSE PRESS

NEW YORK § TORONTO

For My Husband
You expand me beyond my wildest dreams

This book is dedicated to children and grown-ups alike. I invite you to make this journey your own -- as a child, as a grown-up, or perhaps, as the child within all grown-ups. I invite you to dream of peace, to practice peace, and to remember that, regardless of what anyone says, you can make a difference.

I

For as long as I can remember, I've been worried about the world.

Flowers get along. Puppies get along. Snails get along. Babies get along. So...why can't everyone else get along? There are cities where they start to fight on Monday, end on Sunday and then begin all over again on Monday. For some families, it's right in their backyard. Bullets zip through their windows, bombs come down on their heads, darkness falls even when it's day. The children don't have clean water to drink, clothes to wear, or a school to go to in the morning. The world calls it "war." I call it crazy.

On one particular night, not so very long ago, the possibility of a New War had people nervous and fidgety. This included me. Unhappy thoughts made figure eights in my head and they wouldn't go away. How would war stop people from hating each other more than they had ever hated before?

More than ever, I wanted to fall asleep and find peace.

At least once a week, and this has happened since as long as I can remember, I dream of an angel named Peace -- the most beautiful creature I've ever seen. Peace has a body of soft, thick, layered feathers, large see-through wings, sparkling hazel eyes and a smile as brilliant as a sunset. In my dream, Peace beckons me forward, choosing me to play with, making me a friend. When I see Peace, all my worries, fears and harsh thoughts melt away.

If I had one wish, it would be that Peace could be with me all the time. I often think about where Peace lives and if I'll be able to find Peace one day when I'm awake.

I had finally fallen asleep when a loud rap-tap-tap on my door woke me up. I looked at my clock. It was one in the morning! I threw on my robe and woolly slippers -- the ones with a chunk of the right heel missing, thanks to my dog Ange -- and headed for the door. I had named my dog Ange (pronounced 'onje') because it means "angel" in French. She hadn't been an angel the day she had bitten the heel off, however.

"Open up," a man's voice encouraged from the other side.

I lowered my voice and hoped it would make me sound taller than I was. "Who's there?" I replied.

"Luther's my name," he responded sincerely. "I've been sent to get your help."

"Help?"

"To set Peace free."

"The angel Peace?" I asked, astonished.

"That's right. Aren't you Peace's friend?"

"Yes, I guess I am."

"Good." He sounded relieved.

"What's happened?"

"Peace has been taken prisoner, locked in an unbreakable glass box, and can't get out."

"Oh, no," I said in disbelief.

"Oh, yes. Peace's wings have started to droop. Peace needs you before it's too late."

Something in the way he spoke convinced me he was truthful, and although my parents told me never to open the door to strangers, his voice didn't feel strange at all. I cracked the door a little to check him out. Lo and behold, there stood a large, handsome brown bear. He wore a black suit, an ironed white shirt and a thin, black tie tied neatly around his neck. In his paw was a handkerchief which he used to pat his forehead.

"We have to hurry," he said. He extended his paw through the open door to shake my hand.

I couldn't believe how soft and furry his paw felt. It made me want to pet his entire arm. Instead I stared, speechless. I had never spoken with a bear before.

"Yes, you have," Luther said.

What? He read my mind! I suddenly realized Luther looked exactly like the teddy bear my Aunt Rosie had given me when I was three years old. I had talked to that bear all the time.

"Where are we going?" I finally blurted out.

"To find the Three Keys."

"The Three Keys?" I repeated.

Luther sighed. "To unlock the box where Peace is captured. Peace needs to be free. It's the only way."

"Why me?"

Luther gazed past my concern and into my soul. "You care about Peace, don't you?"

I nodded. "But how

do I know you're telling the truth?"

"You could ask me something about Peace to make you believe."

I thought for a second about the angel from my dreams. "What color is the angel's Peacedust?"

The big bear didn't even stop to think. "Gold with black sparkles."

I opened the door all the way. I wanted to go even though I knew I should stay.

"How about a glass of cold milk? And a chocolate chip cookie before you leave?"

Luther took my hand and pulled me out the door. "No time for that."

We ran down the hallway, out the kitchen door, and into a reddish-brown forest that lay beyond. Never before had there been a reddish-brown forest outside my door. Luther pointed to a carved log canoe. It hovered an inch above the ground under a sleepy pine tree.

"Jump in," Luther said.

The flying boat had a wide smile on its bow that grinned at me. That, along with the bittersweet taste in my mouth, reminded me I hadn't brushed my teeth before I left.

"Luther, I want to help the angel Peace. I really do. But I have a big day tomorrow. And I have to get some sleep."

"You'll be back before you know it. I promise."

With that, my feet climbed into the canoe with great determination. Luther smiled, picked up two oars from the floor of the boat and began to paddle. We lifted high off the ground and into the sky. Luther reached in front of me, pulled a seatbelt out from the canoe's side, yanked it across my tummy and fastened me in.

"Our final destination is The Mountain Where Dreams Are Made. It's my home." He had a magical tone in his voice that could convince anyone to do anything. It certainly was convincing me. Then he added, "I'm king there."

"I've never met a king before."

"Do you want to know why I'm king?"

I nodded.

"Because I've seen the dream of peace. Now I'm supposed to show it to you."

Our clear, calm night turned into layers of dense, gray fog.

"There's nasty weather ahead," Luther announced. "We're near the City of Right and Wrong, and the air is always bumpy there. They haven't seen much sun in years. Hold tight."

"The City of Right and Wrong? That's a funny name."

"It used to be called Shalom, which means "peace." But they've tied themselves in a terrible knot with all their fighting and disagreeing. They can't move anything forward, not even an inch. They may be near the point of no return."

I could hardly hear him over the roar of the wind. "What's that?"

"That's when there's so much against-ness they can't keep the goodness alive. You know what happens next."

"No, I don't."

"The Cube of Bitterness eats them," he whispered.

I leaned closer so I wouldn't miss a word.

"The Cube is where the 'right ones' go. The ones who think they're right and someone else is wrong. After awhile their 'rightness' grows big inside them -- like when you eat breakfast, lunch and dinner all at once." I touched my stomach and cringed, imagining how fat I'd feel. "All they want to do is punish anyone who disagrees."

The hairs on the back of my neck stood up. The only thing I could say was, "How awful."

"Awful would be good. It gets worse."

"Worse?"

"Once inside the Cube, your eyes can't see beauty." He pointed to a flowing riverbed beneath us. "Your tongue can't taste anything sweet." I thought of a juicy, orange popsicle sliding down my throat and got sad thinking I might never taste it again. "You can't hear the universal heartbeat." He leaned toward me and placed my ear on his chest. Luther's heart was beating so strong, I felt like a drummer was inside my head.

I moved my head away. "What you're saying frightens me."

"The more the Cube eats, the hungrier it gets. If you can't help us free Peace, your world is next."

I gasped. "Oh, no! Maybe we'd better turn back so I can tell someone."

"Too late. The City of Right and Wrong is where the three Keys to free Peace are supposed to be. It's our only chance."

With that, we headed toward the ground. It felt like our canoe was being thrown down a flight of oversized stairs and I grasped the side of the boat so tightly my fingers looked like Luther's claws. I didn't let go until we landed in the craziest city I'd ever seen.

II

Once our canoe came to a full stop and Luther undid my seatbelt, we climbed out. Not only was the city jam-packed with every animal I had seen at the zoo, but there were ropes, walls and barricades everywhere.

Leaning his canoe against a nearby wall, Luther attempted

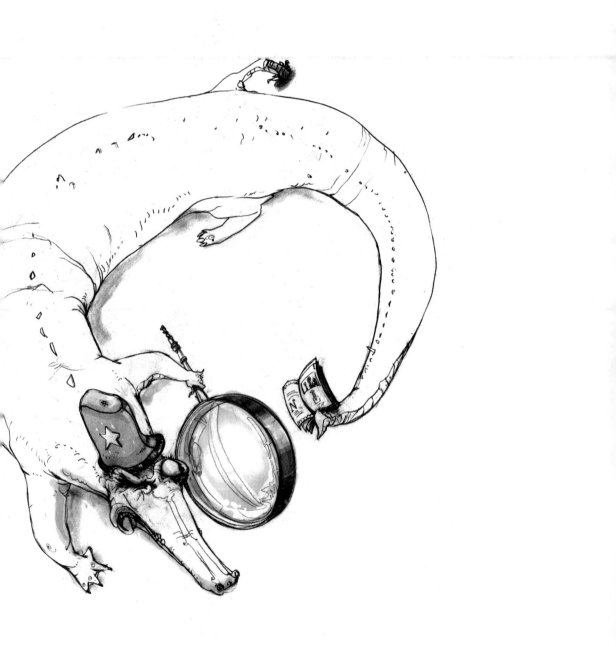

to explain. "The city's been divided over the topic of milk," he commented. "Every animal who likes to drink milk lives over there." He pointed to a tall concrete wall where an armed zebra looked down on us through a pair of gigantic binoculars. Gesturing toward an alligator in a military uniform, he added, "Every animal who hates milk lives over there." The alligator checked a lion's papers with an oversized magnifying glass.

Luther took my hand and pulled me down a narrow cobblestone street crowded by a family of ducks. Each duck carried a grocery bag and rushed in and out of the stores.

"They have to shop before dusk," noted Luther. "Too dangerous after that."

We winded down five more streets, around two more corners, and came to an old brick stadium. Luther marched up to the admission booth, bought two tickets and walked us inside. The animals sat in separate sections marked "I LIKE MILK" and "I HATE MILK," where they booed, hissed and yelled ugly words at the center of the stage. I looked down to the playing field to see what the commotion was about. A vicious tug-of-war was taking place. I had played tug-of-war at camp and thought it was fun, but it was nothing like this.

"We're right to like milk!" an agitated pigmy elephant screamed. He wore one of those tiny French hats my aunt Jacqueline calls a 'beret.'

He pulled on a long piece of rope with five other elephants. Saliva dripped from their mouths and their feet slipped in the mud.

"You're wrong to like milk!" a scrawny donkey at the head of a pack of donkeys shouted back. They all wore white bandanas on their heads to catch their sweat. The lead donkey pulled harder on the rope, his face determined and full of pain.

"We're right! You're wrong!" the elephants said.

"You're wrong! We're right!" the donkeys replied.

Two huge video screens wrapped around the stadium.

The first one showed the years, days and minutes the tug-of-war had been going on: fifty-nine years, ninety-six days, and four minutes. The second screen showed the animals that had been hurt playing the right-wrong game. Some had bandaged hands, others broken legs, many were in body casts.

Without warning, some antelopes, horses, and wolves galloped in. They took sides -- screaming, kicking and bucking at one another. If that wasn't scary enough, a group of giraffes and walruses that couldn't get down the stairs grabbed bricks from the walls and threw them at one another. I watched, terrified, as their world began to come apart.

"Someone's got to help," I called out, ducking as a handful of stones flew over my head.

Luther stood behind me. "There is always hope. Follow me."

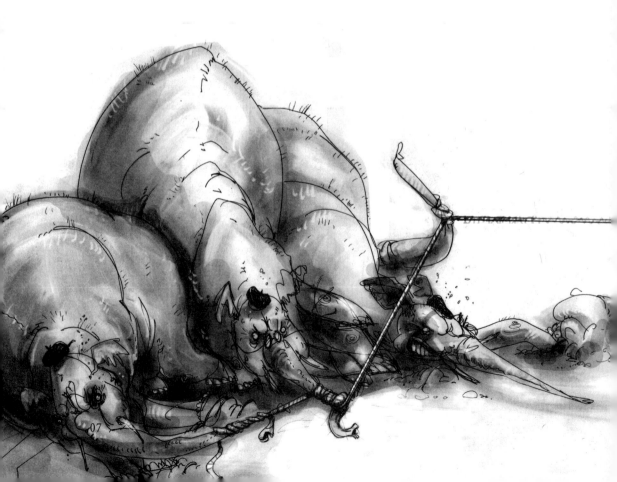

Luther rushed us out of the arena. We zigzagged around parking stalls filled with hay until we reached a nearby square. There, we saw an old Siamese cat with a round wrinkled face, plump body, and a beard of long, white whiskers. He stood on top of a parade float in the shape of a tree. The tree had two hollow knots, like droopy eyes, and branches wrapped around itself as if in prayer. The cat was dressed in a maroon, high-

necked jacket made of silk and three-quarter-length pants. On top of the cat's head was a purple bottle with the word *Acceptance* written across it. The bottle was held in place by a torn, yellow ribbon tied under the cat's chin. The cat was talking through a megaphone to a seemingly random crowd of animals -- parrots, armadillos, sea lions and coyotes -- who had snuck out of their restricted areas to hear him.

"Listen," Luther said.

Come one, come all.

Don't take the fall.

Remember who you are,

And stand tall.

While the cat spoke, the sky grew darker.

It's easy, my friends, to love what you like.

But what if the key is to love what you'd like to bite.

"Oh, sure," a thin coyote mumbled. He eyed a parrot with suspicion. "I don't trust anything that can fly."

The parrot glared at him, flapped its wings and lifted off the ground. The cat swallowed his grin and continued.

It's a no-brainer for a bat to love a bat.

But what if the real adventure is for the bat to love the rat.

And the rat to love the cat.

And the cat to love the muskrat?

"Yeah, right," the red and yellow parrot squeaked. He turned his nose up at a sea lion that stood by his side. "You're always wet and you smell."

"You always talk too much," the sea lion spat back. "There should be a law against noise pollution."

The cat shook his head and went on.

That's why I have an offer you can't refuse.

If you do refuse, you'd have too much to lose.

So buy a bottle of Acceptance and get one free.
Then come on and follow me.

The prospect of something for nothing made the animals move in closer for a better look -- even though they didn't like being near one another.

You see, ladies and gentlemen, I tried Acceptance and got the disease.
Learned to love my neighbor as if he or she were me.
Got the natural rhythm of things in tow.
Realized the right and wrong game really stopped the flow.

The cat jumped off the float, onto the ground and passed around a bottle of his potion. He encouraged each animal to take a sip. The parrot sniffed it to make sure it wasn't milk, then he took a taste.

"Hey," he said, passing the bottle to the armadillo. "I always thought your shell was ugly -- but now I think it's kind of cute."

"That's nice of you," the armadillo replied. He looked at the bottle with distrust and swallowed a swig. "Whoopee!" he hollered. "I used to think you were dumb to eat seeds. Now I see it's sensible." He handed the bottle to a coyote that didn't even bother to check before he took a drink.

"Oh, yeah, baby, I can feel it. You all look too beautiful to eat."

"This stuff is good," the sea lion belched.

This made everyone laugh.

Once you've got Acceptance there's no need to disagree.
No need to blame or judge, not honestly.
You may dig the cat better than the rat.
Or the rat better than the bat.
But that doesn't give you the right to change
The one you like less in the exchange.

This struck a chord in the animals and they crowded around the float. Although a few looked on warily, most held out their hands for a bottle. The cat gestured for us to come over and help. Luther pulled me toward the float.

"Don't we need to find the Keys?" I asked, feeling unsure of whether we had time to help a perfect stranger.

"We do, indeed."

The cat looked over at us and smiled. He tipped his purple bottle hat towards me and introduced himself. "My first name's 'Budd,'" he said, "with two d's. Last name's 'Ha.'" He opened a case of *Acceptance* and handed me four bottles. "Everyone calls me Mister Buddha. You can, too."

"Hello, Mister Buddha," I said.

I took two bottles and handed them to the once-belching sea lion, who promptly grabbed them between her two wet fins.

"Good to see you," Luther said to Mister Buddha as they shook paws.

"Roger that," said the cat as he gave some *Acceptance* to four eager armadillos. He looked down at me and casually noted, "I wondered when you would show."

"You weren't surprised to see me?" I asked. I looked at Luther who just shrugged.

"How long can you stay?" Mister Buddha inquired.

"I'm not sure. We're on a very important mission to find the Three Keys. I have to get them before I go back."

"Three Keys to what?" Mister Buddha asked.

"A glass box that's captured Peace. Peace is being held prisoner, and if we find them we can set Peace free. You don't by chance know where they are?"

Before Mister Buddha could answer, there was a dreadful noise that rumbled in the sky.

Luther pointed at the stadium. "It's here!"

I looked up and wished I hadn't. Over the stadium, in all

its horribleness, was an enormous, shiny, black cube. It was five houses tall and just as wide. Its slick, mirrored surface made it impossible to see inside and its edges were razor-sharp, like a steak knife. On each side were big, red, cracked lips that made a wet, sucking sound and every few seconds a tentacle darted out of the bottom lip. It was gross. It was the Cube of Bitterness.

"Roger that." Mister Buddha gathered his things while the animals scattered in different directions. He tried to appear calm even though I could tell he wasn't.

Thank you, ladies and gentlemen. That's all for today.
We'll be back tomorrow, so come as you may.
Until then, take one teaspoon, morning, noon and night.
And share your Acceptance with everyone in sight.

"Time for some green tea," he suggested. "It's awesome for the aging process." He tapped his high cheekbones with his crinkled, clawed fingers.

I stared at the sky, too frightened to even consider his offer. The Cube's tentacle, which was now inside the stadium, had snatched up every animal that thought he or she was right and someone else was wrong. All were being carried away.

"Wait! My canoe!" Luther screamed.

We turned to see a gang of eye-patched gorillas running down the street with Luther's canoe held over their heads. He ran toward them roaring as loudly as he could. This frightened the gorillas and they dropped the canoe, letting it crash to the ground.

Luther gently picked up his boat. The teeth on the canoe

were chattering rapidly as he held it in his arms. My teeth were chattering too.

"She needs some care," he said with concern. "Go with Mister Buddha. I'll catch up with you later. You must find the Keys."

"But where are they, Luther? What do they look like? Are they large or small? New or old? Hidden or buried?" The possibilities seemed endless.

"You'll know them when you see them. I have to go."

And with that, Luther was out of sight.

"All right." I gathered up my strength. "I'll find them. I will. To set Peace free."

"Roger that. Put these on." Mister Buddha had handed me a pair of goggles. He placed a special set on the tree to protect her long lashes. "Luther and his canoe will be okay." He started up his engines. "I guarantee it." His reassurance touched my heart and I gave him a hug. "Hang on," the old cat said, wiggling out of my embrace.

With that, we were off. And I mean off. His float had dual rocket boosters, which, he said, could reach the speed of light. Before I knew it, the City of Right and Wrong and the dreadful Cube of Bitterness were nowhere to be seen.

III

Mister Buddha captained the float with great expertise, allowing me to enjoy the cool wind on my face.

"My tree is named Bodhi," Mister Buddha said. "She's able to see the love inside all living things." He stroked her nearest branch. "When others can't see it, it makes her sad."

I understood the Bodhi Tree's feelings. I could see the love inside things too. When people shouted at one another, killed insects or flowers, or raised their hands to hit, it made my heart ache, too.

"You're so good-hearted," I said.

The Bodhi tree looked at me and spoke. "If you say you love me but you hate someone else, how can you say you want peace?"

"Think it through," Mister Buddha suggested.

I chewed on the bottom part of my lip and tried to reason it out. "If I love the Bodhi tree...but I don't love you, that means I don't want peace because..."

"Because?" Mister Buddha encouraged.

"Because peace loves all things." Mister Buddha nodded. "So when you hate someone you can't have peace."

"Roger that," Mister Buddha purred. "I couldn't have explained it better myself."

The old cat steered the float toward a patch of white clouds. I looked over at the Bodhi Tree. She batted her long lashes and smiled.

Mister Buddha motioned to me. "Why don't you begin at the beginning," he said good-naturedly. "I'm told it's a good place to start. Tell us why you're here."

I did just that. I told him how the people in my world just couldn't get along. Most didn't believe they could make a difference, but I was determined to find a way. I explained how Luther the Bear had come to me to set Peace free. But we hadn't found the Keys yet and we didn't have much time.

Mister Buddha didn't seem concerned by my urgency. Instead, he waved to a prune-shaped float that passed by. "They're wonderful for morning constitutionals," he sighed.

After what seemed like a long silence, Mister Buddha returned to our earlier conversation. He ran his fingers down his long, white beard.

"Would you like to know why war can never make peace? Like oil and water can never be —"

"Mixed. Because oil floats to the top," I said.

"Roger that." Mister Buddha smiled. "Because hate makes more hate." He steered the float to the right to avoid an approaching rain cloud. "And anger makes more anger." He turned to look at me. "And meanness?"

"Makes more meanness," I tried.

"Roger that," Mister Buddha purred. "So even when the war is over and one side says they've won in the name of peace, there's even more hate than when they began."

"Then what can we do to have more peace?"

"Well..." he began to purr again. "Have you ever been angry with someone for doing something you didn't like and then saw how your anger made the situation worse, not better?"

I thought for a minute. "I get annoyed sometimes with my best friend, Alex." I watched Mister Buddha lower our landing gear. "I hate the way Alex chews bubble gum and leaves it everywhere. He never throws it away. The more it happens, the madder I get until I yell and we start to fight."

"Because you believe it's wrong for Alex to leave the gum around and you're right that it should stop?"

"Yes."

"How does being right make you feel? And the part where you yell and call Alex names?" Mister Buddha peered below for a spot to land.

"Pretty good, at first. Like for twelve seconds."

Mister Buddha chuckled.

"But then bad," I added quickly. "And bad turns to horrible, fast."

"Why?" Mister Buddha shifted gears to slow down our flying float.

"Because I start to feel mean when I hurt Alex's feelings -- stupid that I let a piece of gum ruin our day."

"What other choice might you have when you see Alex put the gum on the table?" He brought the tree to a full stop on top of a hill blanketed in eight leaf clover.

"I could be kind and throw it away myself."

Mister Buddha took a big leap off the float. "Why would that make a difference?" He removed his goggles and offered me his furry paw.

"Because kindness makes more kindness." I took off my goggles and handed them to him. "Alex would still be my best friend and I wouldn't have to look at the gum anymore."

"Roger that. And maybe one day Alex would surprise you and put the gum in the wastepaper basket -- though you wouldn't care by then."

I thought of other things I didn't like, such as girls and boys who were snooty, and grown-ups who never had time to help their children with their homework.

"It's not easy to be nice when I don't like something," I said, jumping down beside Mister Buddha. "Not easy at all."

"Roger that." He took our gear and stashed it in a secret compartment on the side of the float. "But that's everyone's responsibility." He began to walk fast -- for his age -- down the hill, plodding through the clover.

"What is?" I followed in quick pursuit.

"To watch one's thoughts and stop the urge to hit back." He turned and headed up the next hill, lengthening his stride. "War happens when people won't agree to disagree. Until we can accept our differences, there will never be peace."

"Never?" I felt worried.

"Never. Now let's have that cup of tea."

IV

In the time it took to walk to Mister Buddha's favorite restaurant and sit down at his favorite table, I had accepted I was on an adventure that knew where it was going -- even if I didn't.

The restaurant was called the Roomy Tea Garden because of all the space between the tables. Fields of flowers surrounded each one: giant orange daffodils, tall, yellow sunflowers and graceful off-white roses. Large lanterns, in the shape of teabags, provided the light.

"This is where animals who drink my *Acceptance* come to dine. It is a place beyond right and wrong where the sun always shines,"

Mister Buddha said.

I took a moment to breathe in the sweet smell of this wonderful place. Everything here flowed: the grass, the air, even the waiters who drifted between their customers. My thoughts were interrupted by the arrival of a ferret who told me his name was Mahma. Dressed in a white sheet and worn leather sandals, Mahma carried an open sack filled with tiny books. On his nose was a pair of old, wire-rimmed glasses that slid down his snout. He placed his hands in a prayer position to greet me, then bobbed his head up and down.

"Mahma is my best friend," Mister Buddha said, placing his arm around him. "I am certain he can help you find the Keys to set Peace free."

Because of his size, or lack of it, Mahma was given six colored pillows, provided by the Tea Garden staff, to stand on so he could see us better. He was the most adorable creature I had ever seen -- even though his cheeks were red and scratched. As our tea was poured, I asked what had happened to him.

"A rat named Jack lives in a house across from me," he began. Mahma dunked his normal-sized tea bag into his large teacup, which took a lot of strength and skill. "He considers me his enemy and says I'm too refined. I consider him my neighbor, despite our many differences."

Mister Buddha gave him a knowing nod.

"He looks for ways to harm me," said Mahma, sipping his tea. "I look for ways we can live in greater harmony,"

"Why does Jack the Rat hate you so much?" I asked.

"Many, many, years ago, his great, great grandfather told his grandfather that ferrets were their enemy."

"Why?" I looked to Mister Buddha to see if he already knew the answer.

"Because we like different clothes, eat different food and practice different faiths," Mahma replied. "I invited Jack the

Rat for a cup of tea the other day." Mahma adjusted his wire-rimmed glasses that were dangerously close to sliding off his nose. "Would you like to hear what happened? Then I'll look for your Keys. Perhaps they are here."

That news cheered me up. I was worried about Peace and how I'd set Peace free.

"I live in an all-rat neighborhood," Mahma said. "There are two Swiss chalets, five Cheddar cheese cottages and a bunch of Muenster townhouses. My home is non-dairy in theme."

Mister Buddha and I laughed.

"It's a simple grass hut like you might find in a jungle, except the roof is always covered in goop."

"Eggs," Mister Buddha explained. "Jack the Rat throws them late at night when Mahma's asleep."

"That's terrible," I said, clenching my hand into a fist. Then I remembered what Mister Buddha had taught me about the importance of not hitting back. I uncurled my fingers.

"I was sitting cross-legged on the floor of my home," Mahma continued. "I had just begun to sing a song my ancestors taught me when the front door flew open and Jack the Rat burst in. He wore green and black hunter's pants with a shirt and hat that matched. He demanded that I 'stop the racket.'

"I opened my eyes and smiled. 'Hello, Jack. That's a nice hat you have on today,' I commented.

"'Weirdo,' Jack the Rat replied. He flicked my left cheek with his thumb and middle finger. 'We don't like weirdos here.'

"'Why don't you sit down, Jack?' I got up and walked toward my kitchen, offering to make him a cup of tea.

"Jack the Rat broke out into a ream of cruel laughter.

'Sewer water!' he hollered.

"He blocked my path and flicked my right cheek with his thumb and forefinger. Then he ran past me and knocked my teapot on the floor. I picked the teapot up and placed it back on my little stove. Jack the Rat grabbed a dishtowel off the kitchen counter, darted behind me and slapped me on my back.

"'Here, Jack. Let me help you finish what you've begun.' I unwrapped the white sheet that covered my body and showed

Jack the Rat my bare chest. It's quite bony and small. 'If it will make you feel better, hit me as hard as you want.'

"This took Jack the Rat by complete surprise. He dropped the dishtowel along with his jaw.

"Suddenly, the sky darkened and a shadow covered the rat's face. There was a loud, rumbling sound. We both ran to the window and looked up. The horrible Cube of Bitterness was over my house and its big, scary, black surface was like a mirror in a fun house. It made us look large and very easy to see. Its long, nasty tentacle darted out of a pair of wet lips and headed our way.

"'We'd better run, Jack.'

"But it was too late. The tentacle punched a hole through my roof and blocked the door. It looked at each of us, then made a beeline for Jack the Rat.

"Jack the Rat screamed and tucked his tail between his legs.

"I threw myself between the tentacle and Jack the Rat, blocking the creature's ability to wrap itself around Jack the Rat and carry him away. Every move the tentacle made, I was there first.

"This scary dance went on for quite awhile, until the tentacle, frustrated, went after me. But the second it touched my skin, it stopped. You see, when only love is in your veins, the Cube of Bitterness has no power.

"The tentacle grew weak. It lay in my hand and let me stroke it until it fell asleep. But its rest was short-lived. Through the hole in my roof, a bucket of spit-water fell on the tentacle and awakened it again. The Cube of Bitterness yanked it back into one of its lips, like a sling shot returning to its owner's hand, and tore off as fast as it had arrived.

"Jack the Rat and I heaved a sigh of relief. With his knees still trembling, Jack walked over, took off his hat and placed it on my head. He adjusted it until it fit me perfectly.

"'Thank you, Jack. I'm honored to wear it.'

"Jack the Rat turned, raced out of my house, leaped across the street and into his home. That's the last I've seen of him."

I pushed my teacup away. "Why did you have to help him?" I asked. "All he's ever done is call you names, egg your house, and make you feel bad."

Mahma reached into his pocket, took out three apricot lollipops and passed them around. "Jack the Rat wasn't born a bad rat." He dunked his lollipop into his drink and took a sip. "While there are unfair laws and unkind creatures, at the beginning, we're all divine."

Mister Buddha stroked his whiskers, and nodded. "Every great religion says so. Including mine."

Mahma licked his lollipop up one side and down the other. "So the quicker we accept we are One, the sooner we'll have the experience we most seek."

"Peace," Mister Buddha said. He smiled as he finished his drink.

Mahma bobbed his head up and down, pushing his glasses back up on the bridge of his nose. "Which is why I haven't hated another living thing in over forty ferret life spans."

"Nor I in a thousand Siamese New Years," added Mister Buddha, licking his lips and beginning to purr.

"I believe one day Jack the Rat will come to respect me." Mahma removed the teabag from his cup. "Perhaps today was that day."

In the face of such kindness, there was little left to say. We silently began to search for the Keys. For over an hour, Mister Buddha and I looked in keyholes, under doormats and in mailboxes -- Mahma dashed under each cheese house, ran over each roof, and searched every garbage can. The Keys were nowhere to be found.

Back at the Roomy Tea Garden, we rested our tired feet.

"How did you two meet?" Mahma asked. He slid his glasses

to look at a small note the restaurant had brought

ngerine tray.

e City of Right and Wrong," Mister Buddha replied.

"With Luther the Bear," I added.

"He's a great bear," said Mahma, placing the note on the table.

"You know Luther?" I asked, astonished.

"Indeed I do. He paid me a visit once and we had a marvelous time. Is he going to show you his dream?"

"If I ever see him again." I placed my head in my hands.

Mister Buddha put his arm around me. "Cheer up and remember your plan."

"To find the Keys to set Peace free. But I don't even know where to look."

Mahma pushed the note toward Mister Buddha. "If this is right, you're due at the Sea of Forgiveness in an hour."

I sat up straight in my chair. "The Sea of Forgiveness? What's that?"

Mister Buddha studied the note. "Of course. The Keys must be there. Can you make it in time?" he asked, leaving my own question unanswered.

Mahma took out a worn map from his bag, studied it, then bobbed his little head up and down.

"If we take the underground highway we can."

"Underground? That doesn't sound good to me," I said, concerned.

But there was no time for further discussion. The next thing I knew, Mahma and I were seated on a giant maple leaf, sliding down a ferret hole on what felt like the roller coaster ride of my life.

V

When my eyes got used to the dark, I discovered we were on a rodent highway deep beneath the earth -- lit by old-fashioned street lamps with pale, yellow lights. Two squirrels in acorn cars and a mouse on a big piece of kibble sped by us. We flew past exit signs for Newt York City, Ferret Frisco and Mouseport. Sometimes we hit big bumps in the road that gave us a jolt. I guessed that they didn't have road repairmen here like we did at home.

"I've read a lot about your civilization," Mahma said.

"You have?" I wondered if my fanny could take this part of the adventure much longer.

"There's one thing that confuses me more than anything else." He gestured ever-so-slightly and the leaf took an exit marked Gopherstine. "Why is it humans say they want peace but so few are willing to do what it takes to get it? And the few who are willing are killed, or in some way harmed."

Although this was a hard question, I liked how Mahma trusted I might have the answer.

"Maybe we don't understand what we have to do."

"Perhaps. Or perhaps you don't realize that peace is hard work. It takes energy, determination and skill. It's a discipline, like any other. No different than when you learn to ride a bike or study how to use a computer. No different than when you become good in a language or great at a sport."

"No different than when you draw the same thing over and over again, until you get it perfect," I added.

"Exactly. Think of peace as a muscle that has to be strengthened or else it grows weak." Mahma adjusted his glasses around his ears.

We flew down a passageway, up the other side, and popped back up above the ground.

"To be good at peace, you must practice," Mahma said.

"And practice some more," I added. The maple leaf came to a stop.

"Because practice..." Mahma continued.

"Makes perfect!" we said together. We rolled off the leaf in a wave of laughter.

The leaf smiled too, then quickly returned to the sky in search of its next fare. Mahma seemed tired, so I picked him up and put him on my shoulders. I knew he could guide our travels from there. He wrapped his little legs around my neck, removed a notebook and pencil from his bag, adjusted his spectacles and began to write.

"Are you doing homework?" I asked, stepping over a rock.

"In a way. It's an article for our newspaper, *The Ferret Gazette*. I'm calling it, 'Be the change you want to see in the world.'"

"Cool title."

He bobbed his head up and down. "Are you?"

"Am I what?"

"Doing the things you think will make the world a better place?"

I considered my answer carefully. "I want to. I work hard. I try to learn from my mistakes. If someone needs help, I do what I can for them even if I don't feel like it." I walked up and over a sandy dune and stopped to catch my breath.

Mahma jumped up and stood on my shoulders. "I would call that living by example. No wonder you were chosen to set Peace free."

My nostrils had become stuffed on our underground journey, but now they were clearing as the salty smell of the sea began to fill the air.

"The Sea of Forgiveness," Mahma said longingly, staring at the ocean that lay ahead. "Well, I'll be..." He pointed down the way.

I gazed down the beach as two large, hazy figures appeared. They were heading in our direction.

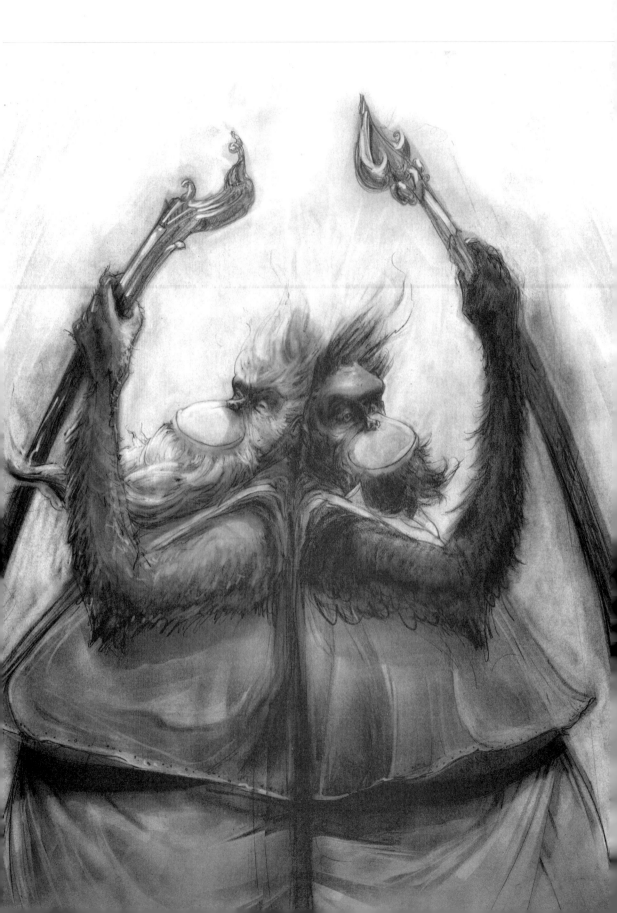

Mahma put his notebook and pen away. "Two of the nicest orangutans you'll ever meet. They even dress a bit like me." He pointed to their white, cotton robes and black belts tied around their waists. Each one held a weathered, wooden walking stick. "The orangutan on the left is Mo. On the right is Chris. They share the same father but have different mothers. Even though they lead separate tribes, they use any excuse they can to be together."

"And today I'm their reason?"

"You are indeed. They've been asked to ferry you across the Sea of Forgiveness to find the Keys."

VI

After hellos were exchanged and we dipped our feet in the warm, grainy seawater, Mahma got ready to leave. The sun had set and the stars were out.

"It was a pleasure to travel with you," Mahma said. He patted me on my ankle. "Please set Peace free so the Cube of Bitterness will never triumph. Only then can our world live in harmony."

I picked him up and held him in my arms. "I will, Mahma. I promise."

He kissed me on my cheek. "Then perhaps we'll meet again."

With that vote of confidence, Mahma leaped to the ground, scurried down the beach and dropped into a hole destined to take him home.

"We'd better get started," Chris said.

"But where's your boat?" I asked.

"Can't you see?" Chris grinned at Mo.

Mo pointed to the stars that shone brightly. I looked and looked until I saw the shape of a hippo with a sail on its back.

"It's waiting for our whistle," Chris suggested.

At that, the three of us put our fingers to our mouths and blew. The boat left its heavenly mooring and appeared right in front of us. Mo and Chris helped me on, and with the aid of a big burst of wind, we set sail on the sea named Forgiveness.

Our raft sailed through the night. Even though the sea was rocky, I felt calm -- except for the loud, gurgling sounds my stomach was making.

"You must be hungry," Mo said. He handed me a piece of funny-looking flat bread. "Bakes itself without an oven." I nibbled on a piece and liked it. "I call it crunchy pita bread."

"Try this," Chris offered.

He handed me a tasty wafer with a glow around it. I liked it, too. Between bites of Mo's crunchy pita and Chris's glowing wafers, I told them about my worries that people couldn't get along and how, with Peace unable to get free, the horrible Cube of Bitterness grew more powerful by the day.

"We understand your worries," Chris said.

"Our brothers and sisters need peace too," Mo added.

The sun peeked its head over the sea. Splashing and flapping occurred all around us, and soon, hundreds of creatures from the sky and sea appeared -- every kind imaginable: barracudas, dolphins, sharks and marlins -- seagulls, hawks, doves and canaries too.

"Good morning, Brothers and Sisters." Mo held his stick up in the air.

"Gather close," Chris encouraged.

The fish jumped out of the water and took seats on waves that became oversized armchairs. The birds plopped down on wind that molded into couches. It looked as if we were in a movie

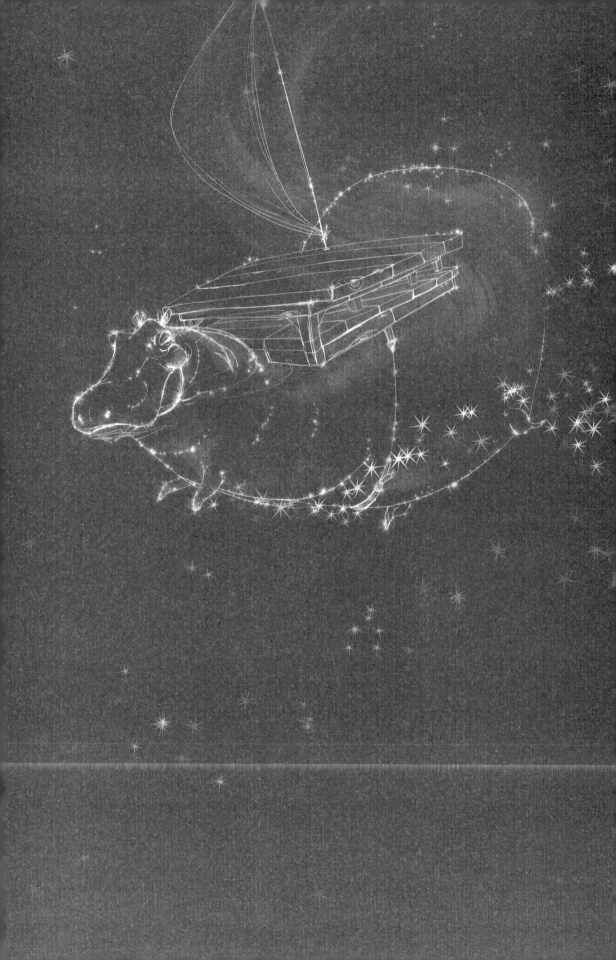

theatre on the sea.

"We feel blessed to be here today," Chris beamed as he stroked the wings of a seagull. "Blessed to behold so many creatures, large and small."

This was answered by sounds of appreciation.

"Word of your challenges has spread across the land," Mo said. "Fish hurting birds, and birds hurting fish, Brothers and Sisters."

A barracuda held up his fin which had a big, nasty scab under it. "You would bite back, too. Look what a pelican did to me."

"Wait a minute!" a hawk squawked. He waved his bandaged leg in the air. "A walrus tried to nibble on me while I was out finding food to feed my family." This was answered with a mixture of grunts and squeals.

"We understand your pain," Chris answered. "We understand your suffering. But you must understand each other's pain and suffering, too."

"You have been given a promised sky," Mo said. "And a promised sea. In return, only one thing is asked of you."

"To give of ourselves for the good of others?" a silver dolphin squeaked.

"That's right, Brother Dolphin." Mo patted his shiny nose.

Chris turned to the barracuda. "So the next time, Beloved, a pelican mistakes your head for a rock, help him understand his error." The barracuda nodded.

Mo embraced the hawk. "The next time your food is near a family of walruses, Noble Sister, fly a little further out to sea so the momma won't feel afraid. You have a big family, too. I'm sure you understand." The hawk squawked her agreement.

Chris held his walking stick up in the air. "A good life -- is when we learn to live together."

This brought the audience to their feet.

An hour later, after Mo had heard each fish's problem and every bird's complaint, and Chris had agreed to let six fish and six birds travel with him as his students, we were alone again.

"Are you ready?" Chris asked. Mo combed Chris' long, thin hair that had been tangled by the ocean breezes.

"For what?" I asked.

"A swim," Mo answered, letting Chris bathe his tired feet.

"To be honest," I admitted, "I'm afraid of the ocean."

"I think I can help." Mo stared across the rocky waters and up at the sky. With a wave of his bushy arm, he calmed the water in front of our raft until it was still.

"Whoa!" I exclaimed.

Chris smiled, took my hand and helped me step off the boat. I closed my eyes, certain I would fall in and drown, but my feet were met by water as firm as land.

"We'll see you when you get back," Chris said.

"From below," Mo added.

"How will I breathe?" I swallowed nervously.

Chris held my face in his hands. "With the help of that which breathes within you. The Keys to set Peace free are buried at the bottom of the sea."

Okay, I thought...*I have to set Peace free.*

I took a large breath, held my nose tight, and dove in. Mo and Chris had kept their promise -- under the water I could somehow breathe. My eyes were open and I could see everything clearly. As I swam toward the bottom of the ocean floor, I began to have the strangest sensation. I wanted to be nice to every person I'd ever been angry with or hated...every person I had thought was mean, unfair, or just plain wrong. Their stories appeared before me.

I saw my cousin, Jerry, who had picked on me when I was four. He had pulled my hair and called me "Big Ears" which made me feel ugly and small. I hated him for it. Then I saw his

older brother, Jimmy, who had teased Jerry the very same way.

In the sea, I saw my school bus driver, Sam, who snapped at me in the mornings when I didn't sit down immediately. He was sad and mad about his wife dying and didn't have much happiness left to share. But I never knew that part of his story before.

Then I saw all of the bullies in all of the schoolyards all over the world...the ones who pushed nice kids around at recess for no good reason. I felt how nervous they were about their looks and how worried they were that they wouldn't get to the next grade. Their fear was the glue that held them together.

The more I saw, the more I wanted to understand, but my visions were interrupted by the sight of three shiny objects that glittered at the bottom of the sea.

"The Keys! The Keys!" I exclaimed. Bubbles poured out of my mouth.

I swam toward the bottom as fast as I could, dreaming of how I would set Peace free, but I must have misjudged the distance. The next thing I knew, I hit my head on the hard, black sand. My eyes started to close, my head dropped to my chest, my body curled up in a little ball.

"Forgiveness," a voice said. It sounded wise and echoed in my head.

With the little strength I had left, I looked around to see who was there. But all I saw was water.

"Forgiveness," I repeated. I watched seven bubbles shoot out of my mouth and up to the water's surface.

"It's how to unlock your love again."

That was all I remember before I fell into a deep, deep sleep.

VII

A gentle wind must have tickled my face because when I awoke, my nose itched. While I was happy I was no longer underwater, I was sad to see that Chris and Mo were nowhere to be found. And...I felt angry I had missed my chance to find the Keys to set Peace free.

I stood up and took a look around. I was in the center of a shape that curved up steeply on two sides, like a half moon. It was pale yellow and had a cold, glassy surface. I wrung out my nightclothes and looked over the edge. All I could see from my perch -- which was at least five ladders off the ground and way too high to jump off of, were cactuses and orange hills.

"Hello...is anyone here?" I called out.

"Why wouldn't someone be here?" a grouchy, female voice replied. "I'm right here -- to your left and at the top."

I followed her voice and ran up the hill, gripping the side tightly to make sure I didn't slide. When I reached the top, I saw my new acquaintance -- a round wooden sleigh in the shape of a horse. She flared her nostrils with a sour look on her face.

"Hop on," the sleigh instructed. "You're late. What is it with you humans and time?"

"I'm late?"

"Well, hello! To ride the Crescent."

"I'm in a Crescent?" I stepped back and looked around again.

"Do I have to explain everything?" The sleigh placed her ears back. "You're on the surface of a Crescent," she snarled. "It's the most famous one on the planet and it's an honor to work here. Climb on, it's now or never."

Although I was a bit offended by her grumpiness, I didn't want to make her even grumpier, so I sat down and held on to her neck. We whooshed up one side and down the other, coming to a stop in the middle of the Crescent.

"Ah will be here shortly," the sleigh said. Her tone was one of respect.

"Ah?" I questioned.

"From the Land of La."

"Ah, from the Land of La?"

"Didn't you hear me the first time?" she snapped. "The reason you're here must be an important one. Ah only sees people one month a year."

"And this wouldn't be that time?"

"Very impressive. You put two and two together."

The sleigh's remarks made me bite my lip. I didn't know how much more I could swallow without talking back. Then I had the oddest thought. It must be tough to go up and down hills all day with perfect strangers. That idea changed the way I felt and my dislike instantly turned to like.

"Can I ask one more question before you go?" I said.

"If you must."

"I'm looking for Three Keys."

"Big whoopee."

"I think I saw them at the bottom of the sea. But I don't

know where I am -- or how to get back. Can you help me?"

"Do I look like a map?"

"You look like a sleigh."

"Then you have your answer, don't you? Nice to meet you," she said in a sarcastic tone, not even trying to be polite.

"Nice to meet you, too." I wanted to say it like I really meant it. I watched her whoosh down the side of the Crescent, over the tip, and out of sight. "Bye, bye…"

VIII

Once the sleigh had gone, I was alone on the Crescent. After I felt sorry for myself for quite some time, I tried to put all that had happened to me together, but like a puzzle with pieces missing, nothing made much sense.

"Ah-choo," a voice said. This startled me.

"God bless you," I said automatically. I twirled toward the sound, happy to have company again. But no one was there.

"Where are you?" I asked.

"Right here."

"I can't see you." I swung back around.

"Ah-choo."

"God bless you, anyway." I kicked my heels and sat on the shiny surface of the pale yellow Crescent.

"Thank you," said the invisible voice. "Do you need to see me to know me?"

"It would be nice, but I guess not really."

"Good. Let's go then, to the East...before I catch a chill."

At that moment, a star-shaped door opened on the side of the Crescent. "The elevator will take us down. Ah-choo."

"God bless you."

I got up, stepped in, and looked at the buttons. One was marked "desert floor." Before I could push it, the button lit up, the door closed and we descended.

"Are you a ghost?"

"More like an essence."

"Is that like a spirit?"

"Uh-huh."

The elevator stopped and the star door opened again.

"After you," the essence announced.

Together, we stepped out onto a sandy road and started to walk. (At least I *think* the essence was walking.) We were heading in the direction of a pomegranate-red rising sun. I had never hung out with an essence before, and certainly not one with a cold, but I had never done a lot of things until now.

"The sleigh told me your name's Ah. From the Land of La," I said politely.

"Uh-huh. She told me you have been looking for the Three Keys to set Peace free. That's quite an important job. You must be tired."

"Well, now that you mention it, I'm pooped. It's been quite a day -- I mean, night."

"Uh-huh."

Suddenly, I was thrown into the air. Before I could scream, I landed on top of a camel's large hump. The camel stretched its long neck around to look at me, causing me to swallow my surprise. Its eyes were red and its face was covered in bumps.

"His name is Mal'aika. It means 'to help.' I might add that he's allergic to sand."

I added up the odds of a camel being allergic to sand and decided they were long. I patted Mal'aika's neck in an effort to make friends.

"I'm sorry you don't feel well," I said. "Is there anything I can do?"

He looked back at me with a faint smile.

"Even though everything's not going my way, I've decided to make it okay. But thank you."

"So, have you found them?" Ah asked. "The Three Keys to set Peace free?"

My head dropped. "No," I said, almost in a whisper. "I haven't."

"Uh-huh," Ah said, his tone not registering even the slightest disappointment. He climbed on board the camel and took the reins -- I knew this because though I couldn't see Ah, I could feel him. "Then we still have a bit of work to do."

Galloping across the desert plains, the land looked more

and more unhappy. The sand was black and the bushes were dead. There was not a sign of life anywhere. It made me feel lonely all over.

"Uh-huh," Ah agreed, apparently able to hear my thoughts just like Luther the Bear had when I had first met him. "The Cube of Bitterness has been here," Ah continued. "There are only two watering holes left. One's over there and it looks like we have company."

In the middle of the ugliness stood one green palm tree hanging over a small pool of water which was an inviting hue of aquamarine. As the camel made its way to the water and began to drink, Ah and I jumped off to meet our fellow travelers who generously introduced themselves.

They were a charcoal-colored tarantula named Sting, a white rabbit called Ootsy and a sand-colored snake that went by the name of Eyeballs. Sting, Ootsy and Eyeballs were playing cards on the back of a brown turtle they called Speedy. Speedy was fast asleep. I couldn't believe my eyes.

"Are you surprised?" Ah asked.

"I thought these creatures would want to eat each other," I whispered.

"Tall tale," Sting said. He wrapped his long, black, hairy legs around his cards so no one could see. "Pardon me if I butt in, but my hearing's top notch."

"No problem," I replied to the spider.

"We've appreciated each other's differences since the beginning of time," Ootsy said. He moved back and forth on his hind legs, indicating the sand was too hot for his big flat feet.

"The rest of the animals and insects bought into the lie," Sting added. He placed one of his cards on the turtle's back.

"That we couldn't get along." Ootsy thumped his right foot.

"But not us-s-s-s," Eyeballs said with a hiss at the end of his words. He uncurled his slithery body just enough to put two of his cards down and draw fresh ones from the pack.

"Which is why the Cube of Bitterness can't gobble you up," I said. I felt very smart.

"That's right," Sting said. "Is it like that in your world?" He placed his cards in one of his other legs and scratched his hairy, black stomach. "You humans have learned how to get along, haven't you?"

"Not exactly," I said.

"Why not?" Ootsy asked, surprised.

"Because they still use war to solve their problems," Ah said.

The three dropped their cards on the hot sand. "War!" they exclaimed.

"To solve problems-s-s-s?" Eyeballs hissed, shaking his head in disgust.

"Yes," I said.

"But aren't you bound by heavenly law like we are?" Ootsy retrieved his cards and placed one on the turtle's back.

I looked toward where I thought Ah was, perplexed.

"To respect all living things. It's our promise," Ah explained.

"All living things-s-s-s," Eyeball said, with that hiss at the end of his words again. "That's the deal."

I sat down next to Sting. "But sometimes don't we have to fight to stop worse things from happening?" I asked.

"How in heaven's name would it help to hurt someone else's child?" Sting replied. His five spider legs shook from the thought.

"Answer that," Ootsy demanded, thumping his right foot to make his point.

"I can't," I said.

Eyeballs stretched out his neck so our noses were an inch apart. "Because it couldn't," he said, swallowing his hiss.

"Never," Speedy said, thrusting his sleepy head out from under his shell.

Sting wrapped his long, black legs around himself. "No way."

"Ah-choo," Ah sneezed.

"God bless you," everyone answered.

Ah blew his nose. "I'm afraid it's time for us to go," Ah said.

I climbed back up on Mal'aika's back. "It was nice to meet all of you."

"Visit us anytime." Sting shuffled the deck between two of his five arms and then gave it to Ootsy.

Ootsy took the cards from Sting and began to deal a new hand. "Where are you going?" Ootsy asked.

"To find the angel Peace," Ah said.

"And set Peace free," I said, "if we can find the Three Keys."

Speedy reached his neck out farther. "Will you pass the Waterfall of Mercy?"

"We will," Ah confirmed.

"Oooooh," Ootsy thumped both feet.

"La, la's-s-s-s," Eyeballs said with that hiss.

"Take your handkerchief." Sting reached his five legs out and stretched one forward to shake my hand. "You'll need it."

IX

Four steep sandy hills and two long, flat miles later, Ah was almost finished with the story of his people's search for the Holy Land. He had begun telling the story to take my mind off my low spirits from not finding the Three Keys.

"Did they find the Holy Land, Ah?" I couldn't wait for the answer any longer.

"Uh-huh. But not in the place they thought they would. Kind of like your Keys. It seems the Holy Land was any place where love was present. All they had to do was open their hearts and they would be there."

"You mean my home is a Holy Land?" I giggled, tickled by the thought.

"Is it filled with love?"

"Lots of it."

"Uh-huh." Ah laughed. He joined in my delight.

The sun burst through the cloudy skies and there, in all its greatness, stood the Waterfall of Mercy. It was a lot closer than we had thought. Deserts can be odd that way. The waterfall had silver water that fell in the shape of giant teardrops.

"Ohhhh," a teardrop moaned.

"Nooo," another teardrop cried.

"Don't," another sobbed.

"Do you know why the Waterfall cries?" Ah asked.

I shook my head.

"For the part inside us all that hurts. The Waterfall cries when we hurt ourselves and when we hurt each other." I could hear Ah crying. Then he sneezed again, "Ah-choo."

I felt a tear in my eye, too. "God bless you."

He blew his nose and continued: "The water's neither hot nor cold. They say it answers questions for those who touch it. I'm sure you have some."

I nodded.

"Go on then."

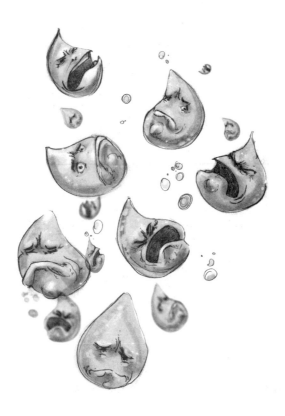

With Ah's encouragement, I knelt before the wall and passed my hands under the gooey water. It felt like liquid Silly Putty.

"Okay...Waterfall of Mercy, why is it so hard for people to get along?" I wiped the tear from my eye.

As promised, the Waterfall spoke in a tone as deep as a cello's. "Inside each of us are good thoughts and hurtful thoughts."

"And we have to pick which thoughts to follow?" I wiped my nose on my sleeve.

"Each and every day."

"That's what I learned from Mister Buddha. And what Mahma showed me. And what Chris and Mo told the birds and the fish. And what Ah believes, and my mother and father too."

"They are good teachers then," the Waterfall replied.

"Then I want to love like you do, Ah." I turned to where I felt he was. Ah, in all of his greatness, didn't answer. "Like Mister Buddha, Mahma, Luther, Chris and Mo do -- even when it's not easy." I placed my hands back in the water again. "Waterfall, do you think I can learn to love instead of hate?"

"Do *you*?"

"I have to if I want peace."

"That was the hope."

"Whose hope?"

"The hope of the One whose love for you never sleeps."

"Like my parents?"

"That's right."

The thought of being loved so much made my heart swell like a balloon, and soon I couldn't tell my tears apart from those of the Waterfall of Mercy

X

Later that day, Ah and I stopped at a second watering hole so I could eat a cactus sandwich and drink a large cup of palm tree juice. There, Ah received a message from a pink goose who had been sent by a magic carpet (who was under the weather that day) to tell us that someone was waiting at the next crossroads to take me to the angel Peace. It seemed that Peace had grown even weaker and the time we had left to save the angel was short. If that wasn't bad enough, the Cube of Bitterness had been seen six more times and everyone was frightened.

I stood at the crossroads, worried again, not sure what to do next. Then I heard Ah say, "I have a surprise. Unless I'm mistaken, there's your friend."

I looked ahead and couldn't believe my eyes. Luther the Bear and his flying canoe were sailing toward me. The minute they landed, I ran into his arms and held him tight. His silky fur dried my forehead, which was moist with sweat from the desert heat.

"It's time, Luther," Ah said, "to show your dream."

Luther put out his paw and helped me into his canoe. The canoe turned, smiled at me and lifted off the ground.

"Thank you for everything, Ah," I said.

"Sallallahu alayhi va sallam," Ah replied.

"May the blessings and peace be upon you," Luther translated as we rose into the sky. "We'll circle seven times. In Ah's world, it's a way to show respect."

"I'd like that." I gulped, swallowing my sniffles.

Luther made our last circle and steered to the North. "You've found the Three Keys, haven't you?"

"I'm sorry, Luther. I don't think I have. I believe I've failed Peace," I said, nearly in tears.

"Nonsense," he replied. "They just weren't where you thought they'd be. Think again."

I thought and I thought and I thought some more, until suddenly, I began to see things in an entirely new way.

What if a Siamese cat with a magical potion had given me one Key? What if a ferret that preached brotherly love had given me the second Key? What if two happy orangutans with a connection to the sea had shown me the third Key? And an essence had helped me put it all together?

What if the Three Keys weren't actual objects I had to find but choices I had to make? To accept people's differences, even when I wanted to be right and make them wrong. To love someone, even when I wanted to hate because I didn't agree with him or her at all. To forgive, even when I wanted to blame and call them cruel names.

"Luther," I exclaimed. "You're right. I did find the Keys!"

"That's wonderful news." He gave me a big thumbs-up.

"But what do I do with them once we find Peace?"

"You'll know when you get there."

As we soared toward The Mountain Where Dreams Are Made, my head spun like a top, with new ideas about how to make the world a better place. First -- all of the principals, teachers and substitute teachers in every school would teach peace. Peace could be right after English, just before history, and not on the days kids have science and math. We would learn to get along from the very beginning and the Cube of Bitterness would have no one to eat.

Then, when every child was studying, learning and practicing peace, grown-ups would have to grow up next. Once they learned to love peace as much as they loved their children, we could feel safe the angel Peace would never get captured again.

"Look," announced Luther. He pointed at a beautiful mountain in the distance. "That's where I live." His voice was filled with pride.

I gazed at Luther's home and began to miss my own.

"You'll be there soon enough. I always keep a promise."

XI

It was standing room only on Luther's mountaintop. Hundreds of other proud bears -- black, brown, golden and white -- had come to see their king's dream. They gathered around a lavender screen made just for that purpose.

Luther's dream was the most wonderful story I had ever been told -- greater than any book I had read or movie I had seen. His dream was about a place where you could be the same or you could be different. It didn't matter. If you had the color of Luther or Mahma's skin, that was great. If you came from the land where Chris and Mo were born, that was cool. If you believed in Ah's Holy Land or liked Mister Buddha's better, that was a-okay.

In Luther's dream, when someone made a mistake (which happened from time to time), the mistake was punished but not the goodness inside the creature. It was understood that darkness could never stamp out darkness, so love was rubbed on everyone's boo-boos like a magical ointment.

Out of consideration for one another, respect became the way to say thank you for all that had been given. Once a year, like a vaccination, everyone received an injection of love as protection from the horrible Cube of Bitterness. On that day, all work stopped and love poured through their veins like maple syrup. Peace was everywhere, which had always been the plan.

As the screen returned to its resting place, there wasn't a dry eye on the mountaintop. Even those bears that had seen it before sobbed.

"Peace is possible, isn't it, Luther?" I asked.

"No ifs, ands, or human buts."

"Thank you, Luther."

I gave him a kiss on his cheek.

"Hang on," he said.

"To what?"

Once again, there was no time for explanations. Luther touched the middle of my forehead and we were back in the City of Right and Wrong -- the place where they had once fought over who liked milk and who didn't like milk.

I looked around the city to see if the Cube Of Bitterness was anywhere to be found. When I realized it was gone, I shrieked with joy. "Yippee!"

Luther took my hand and urged me to hurry. We made our way through the rubble, then he led me behind one of the broken-down walls. There, in a glass box, stood the angel Peace. We had been so close and I never knew it.

Peace looked at me with eyes that could melt the largest glacier. "Hello, dear one," Peace greeted.

I ran up to the box and placed my right hand on it, wishing I could touch Peace. "Are you all right?" I held my breath and waited for Peace's answer.

"I will be. Did you find the Three Keys? My legs are very tired and my Peacedust has started to disappear."

"I did, angel Peace."

"I knew you would." Peace seemed happy.

"But they're not real keys," I explained. I noticed that the lock on the box had no keyholes.

"No, they're not," Peace smiled.

"So...I had to go someplace else."

"And where was that?"

I touched my chest. "The Three Keys are in here."

Peace smiled at me with the tenderness of a dewdrop.

"Then you best put them to work from there."

Determined to set Peace free, I closed my eyes and tried to think of a time when I didn't use the Keys. It was all I could think to do.

A memory popped into my head of a little boy I knew named Charlie and the day I had worked up the courage to ask him to play. Instead of responding the way I wanted him to, Charlie told me he thought play dates were a waste of time. I became hurt and then angry and I wished bad things would happen to him, like flunking his exams. For the rest of the year I told the other kids in our class he was stupid and weird.

With that story in my head, I called Mister Buddha into my heart and asked for his help. He appeared before me, untwisted his long, white whiskers, took out a bottle of *Acceptance* and gave me a sip. The second I swallowed, I felt better. It was okay that Charlie didn't want to play -- he didn't have to like the same things I did. I could always find someone else to be my friend and that would be good, too.

Mister Buddha smiled, tipped his bottle hat and left. Soon, Mahma arrived and sat on my shoulder. We talked about doing unto others as we would want them to do unto us. Just because Charlie didn't do what I wanted was not a reason to hate him. It was still my job to care for him -- even if he didn't seem to care about me. The minute I promised Mahma I would keep my heart open, Mahma vanished too.

Chris and Mo sailed in on a puff of wind. In Chris's hand was a bowl of water from the Sea of Forgiveness. We stared into it and more of Charlie's story appeared. Almost everyday, Charlie ran home from school to take care of his four younger brothers and sisters. That way, his mom, who was ill, could get some rest, and his father, who worked two jobs, wouldn't have to worry. Although he never got to play with the kids at school, he was glad he could help his family as much as he did. Like saying "abracadabra," my hurt feelings disappeared and in their place

was a wishing well of understanding.

"Do you see what I see?" Luther asked.

"What?" I opened my eyes.

"The glass box has disappeared!"

Lo and behold, Luther was right. There was not a trace of
the prison that had once captured Peace. We looked up to the sky
and watched in awe as the angel Peace flew through the air, wings
spread wide. Peacedust fell from the angel and touched every

creature Peace could see, including me.

"You did it!" Luther lifted me up and tossed me in the air. "You used the Three Keys! You set Peace free!" He caught me in his furry arms and I hugged him tightly. "When we open the doors for peace," he beamed, "the world is a better place."

XII

I suppose I shouldn't have been surprised, but I was.

The moment I chose peace and Peace was freed, everything in the city changed. The walls and ropes fell down. The alligators no longer needed to check papers and the armed zebras had no reason to protect their turf. The animals that liked milk were free to drink it anywhere and the ones that didn't like milk were appreciated for their different point of view.

I grinned from ear to ear. Everywhere I looked there were miracles happening. In the square, thousands of animals had gathered to hear Chris and Mo talk about forgiveness. If that wasn't fantastic enough, the line for Mister Buddha's *Acceptance* was over twenty blocks long. Luther had been asked to show his dream and Mahma had become an instant celebrity. The story of his love for Jack the Rat had traveled across the land and everyone wanted to hear it.

I felt a gentle wind blow across my face and I knew this was Ah. He was here to bless the land with the only ingredient that could make it Holy again: love.

In the stadium, where I had once seen the endless tug of war, a huge peace party was underway. Streamers hung from the rafters, balloons floated in the air and music blasted from the speakers. Pandas danced with alligators, llamas with bobcats, coyotes with lions and all of my new friends danced with me.

I did the "Siamese Tea Cup" with Mister Buddha, the "Ferret Two-Step" with Mahma, the "Bear-Hug-Swirl" with Luther, the "Monkey" with Chris and Mo, and sang a song called, "R-E-S-P-E-C-T" with Ah from the Land of La. When I was so tired I couldn't dance another step, I decided to sit down and rest for a minute. I closed my eyes, and without meaning to, I fell asleep.

XIII

When I woke up, I was stunned to see I was under the covers of my bed, my dog Ange snoring at my feet.

"What?" I sat up. "I'm home?"

Ange stared at me, eyebrows raised, as if to say, "Are you nuts?"

"Do you know where I've been?" I tried to shake off my confusion. "It was incredible." I scratched her head. "I met Luther the Bear, flew with Mister Buddha on his Bodhi tree, traveled with a ferret named Mahma, sailed with Chris and Mo on the Sea of Forgiveness, met Ah from the Land of La, saw Luther's dream and found the Three Keys to set Peace free."

Bored, Ange got up and left the room. I looked at my clock. It was six in the morning. Luther had kept his promise. I jumped out of bed, walked over to my desk and sat down in my chair. Clean, white sheets of paper stared up at me and I knew I had to do something with all I had learned.

I picked up my pen and I started to write - and write - and write.

XIV

Incredibly, what I wrote reached many. I told my friends it was because the angel Peace sprinkled Peacedust on my words every night. Some believed me, others just laughed.

With time, my story brought people together from all over the world to study, learn and practice peace. A great gathering had been organized and I had been asked to speak. There were people there of every age -- children, teenagers, mothers, fathers, and grandparents. There were people of every color, too -- brown, black, white, beige and gold. They wore all

kinds of clothing -- suits, dresses, skirts, jeans and shorts. And every kind of headgear -- turbans, baseball hats, yarmulkes, and scarves.

I spoke to the gathering about the journey I had taken to set Peace free. I explained what I had learned from Luther the Bear, Mister Buddha, Mahma the ferret, Chris and Mo, Ah from the Land of La and the angel Peace. I told them that acceptance, love and forgiveness were the Three Keys.

"It's okay not to like what everyone says," I said. "It's okay not to like what everyone does." My heart pounded quickly. "What isn't okay is to hate them for it. Because hate makes more hate -- and nothing good comes from hate."

For a moment, I could see the love inside each person and it captured my breath. "Ladies, gentlemen, children of this precious planet -- join me today to set peace free. Accept your differences, do unto others as you would have them do unto you and forgive them for whatever you feel they have done that is wrong. Perhaps, if you knew their story, you'd understand their pain. Thank you."

I took a small bow and when I raised my head back up, I saw my special friends again. They were gathered at the Roomy Tea Garden for a tea party in my honor.

"God bless you," Mister Buddha and Luther said through Mister Buddha's megaphone.

"We love you," Mahma, Mo and Chris sang out. They held their teacups up in a toast.

"Peace be still," Ah whispered on the gentleness of the dry wind.

The angel Peace handed me a bag of gold Peacedust with black sparkles in it.

"Remember, Dear One: peace begins within. And it is now within you."

With Peace's blessing in my heart and a big smile on my face, I found myself back before the great gathering. I spread my

arms wide and started to fly. I reached down and grabbed hold
of a little boy's hand. He grabbed hold of his mother's hand.
She grabbed hold of her husband's hand and before I knew it,
we were all flying through the air holding hands. We looked like
a long tail on a colorful kite.

     Into the sky we went, sprinkling Peacedust on everyone we
could see. I knew the angel was right. I did a somersault into a
cloud and swooped back out the other side.

     We know where Peace lives and we are making a difference.

Martin Luther King, Jr. (1929-1968)

Martin Luther King, Jr. was one of the most famous and important leaders of the American Civil Rights Movement. He was a Baptist minister and was considered a peacemaker throughout the world for his beliefs in nonviolence and equal treatment for all races. He was the youngest person to ever receive a Nobel Peace Prize. He was assassinated in 1968.

Martin Luther King, Jr.'s most celebrated speech is, "I Have A Dream." Here are some passages from it:

...even though we face the difficulties of today and tomorrow, I still have a dream.

It is a dream deeply rooted in the American dream. I have a dream that one day this nation will rise up and live out the true meaning of its creed: "We hold these truths to be self-evident, that all men are created equal."

I have a dream that one day on the red hills of Georgia, the sons of former slaves and the sons of former slave owners will be able to sit down together at the table of brotherhood.

I have a dream that one day even the state of Mississippi, a state sweltering with the heat of injustice, sweltering with the heat of oppression, will be transformed into an oasis of freedom and justice.

I have a dream that my four little children will one day live in a nation where they will not be judged by the color of their skin but by the content of their character.

I have a dream today!

I have a dream that one day, down in Alabama, with its vicious racists, with its governor having his lips dripping with the words of "interposition" and "nullification" -- one day right there in Alabama little black boys and black girls will be able to join hands with little white boys and white girls as sisters and brothers.

I have a dream today!

Practice Peace
Learn more about Martin Luther King, Jr.

Siddhartha Gautama, (c. 566 – 486 B.C.E.)

Siddhartha Gautama was the historical founder of Buddhism.

When Siddhartha Gautama was born, a seer predicted he would either become a great king or he would save humanity.

Fearing his son would not follow in his footsteps, his father raised Siddhartha in a world of wealth in order to hide him from any experience of human misery or suffering.

However, when Siddhartha saw four sights - a sick man, a poor man, a beggar, and a corpse - he was so filled with sorrow he dedicated himself to finding a way to end human suffering.

He abandoned his former way of life, including his wife and family, and committed himself to a life of yogic meditation.

After many harsh years of learning, he earned the title of Buddha, or "Awakened One." Siddhartha left his seclusion and returned to the world to teach and help free humanity of their suffering.

In Buddhism, a Buddha is any being who has overcome greed, hate and ignorance and is free of suffering.

Buddhists work to overcome darkness by practicing acceptance and compassion. Compassion is a deep awareness of the suffering of others and the wish to relieve it.

Practice Peace
Learn more about Buddhism

Mahatma Gandhi (1869-1948)

"I have nothing new to teach the world. Truth and non-violence are as old as the hills."

Mahatma Gandhi was born in India and educated in law at University College, London. When Gandhi returned to India he found himself treated as a member of an inferior race. He threw himself into the struggle for elementary rights for Indians and began to teach a policy of passive resistance and non-cooperation to effect social and political change. Gandhi became the international symbol of a free India. He lived a spiritual and ascetic life of prayer, fasting, and meditation, an expression of a way of life implicit in the Hindu religion.

Gandhi's death was regarded as an international catastrophe. A period of mourning was set aside in the United Nations General Assembly, and condolences to India were expressed by all countries. In tribute to Gandhi's life, the HH Dalai Lama said:

> I have the greatest admiration and respect for Mahatma Gandhi. He was a great human being with a deep understanding of human nature... Ahimsa or nonviolence is the powerful idea that Mahatma Gandhi made familiar throughout the world. But nonviolence does not mean the mere absence of violence. It is something more positive, more meaningful than that, for it depends wholly on the power of truth. The true expression of nonviolence is compassion...To experience genuine compassion is to develop a feeling of closeness to others combined with a sense of responsibility for their welfare. This develops when we accept that other people are just like ourselves in wanting happiness and not wanting suffering...As Mahatma Gandhi showed by his own example, nonviolence can be implemented not only in politics but also in day-to-day life. That was his great achievement...I believe that it is very important that we find positive ways in which children and adults can be educated in the path of compassion, kindness and nonviolence. If we can actively do this I believe we will be fulfilling Mahatma Gandhi's legacy to us. It is my prayer that, as we enter this new century, nonviolence and dialogue will increasingly come to govern all human relations.

PRACTICE PEACE
Learn more about Mahatma Gandhi

Jesus Christ, also called Jesus of Galilee or Jesus of Nazareth (6-4 B.C.E. to 30 A.D.)

Considered the founder of Christianity, one of the world's largest religions and the incarnation of God according to most Christians, Jesus Christ's influential teachings and deeds were recorded in the New Testament.

Jesus Christ was born in Bethlehem. He worked as a carpenter until his ministry began, around the age of thirty. With his twelve apostles, Jesus inspired people to live a godly life. As he traveled around Israel, he taught with sermons and parables. His most famous sermon was the Sermon on the Mount. There he preached the following ethics:

* Love your enemies
* Do not judge others
* Trust God
* Don't be anxious about the future
* Do unto others as you would have them to do unto you

People who did not agree with Jesus' beliefs accused him of the crime of blasphemy. Jesus was sentenced to death by crucifixion and died on the cross.

During his lifetime Jesus was said to have performed many great miracles -- none as important as his own resurrection.

Jesus' life and death are a celebration of the power and importance of compassion.

Practice Peace
Learn more about Christianity

MOSES (AROUND 1500 B.C.E., HISTORIANS DISAGREE ON ACTUAL BIRTH)

Moses was the legendary Hebrew liberator, leader, lawgiver and historian. He is considered the greatest figure in the Hebrew Bible.

Suffering the abuse of slavery in Egypt, Moses led the Israelites out of Egypt and into the desert. When he reached Mount Sinai he received the Torah from God. Torah means teaching, instruction or law. The most famous words in the Torah are the Ten Commandments, a code for peace and harmony within the community and beyond. The Ten Commandments became the values by which Jews live.

1. Have no other gods.
2. Have no idols.
3. Honor God's name.
4. Honor the Sabbath day.
5. Honor your parents.
6. Do not murder.
7. Do not commit adultery.
8. Do not steal.
9. Do not perjure yourself.
10. Do not covet.

Through God, Moses also bestowed the priestly benediction, the final and key word of which is "Shalom," (Peace). "The Lord bless you and keep you, the Lord make his face shine upon you, and be gracious to you, the Lord lift his countenance upon you and give you peace."

Moses instructed the Jewish people to always offer and seek peace with their enemies.

It is interesting to note that Moses is mentioned more often in the New Testament than any other Old Testament figure and in the Qur'an, he is narrated and recounted more than any other prophet recognized in Islam.

Abraham is a very close second. And, of course, Abraham is regarded as the father of the Jewish faith.

PRACTICE PEACE
Learn more about Judaism

MUHAMMAD THE PROPHET (PEACE BE WITH HIM) (570-632)

Muhammad the Prophet is the central figure to the faith of Islam.

It is said that when the angel Gabriel visited Muhammad as a young man he was commanded to recite verses sent by God. These revelations became his life's calling and through his commitment and dedication he grew to become one of the most respected spiritual leaders of all time, leading a faith based community that has impacted the world.

The words that God spoke to Muhammad were written down and compiled into the Qur'an. Over one billion people presently practice the beliefs of Islam. Islam is a message for the salvation of humanity. It is to save, not destroy people. It is to love, not hate. Here are parts of the speech Muhammad gave during his final Pilgrimage to Mecca:

> Hurt no one, so that no one may hurt you. Remember that you will indeed meet the Lord, and that He will indeed reckon all your deeds... All mankind is from Adam and Eve; an Arab has no superiority over a non-Arab, nor does a non-Arab have any superiority over an Arab. Also a white person has no superiority over a black person, nor does a black person have any superiority over a white person, except by piety and good action. Learn that every Muslim is a brother to every Muslim and that Muslims constitute one brotherhood...Do not stray from the path of righteousness after I am gone.

Other examples of the Prophet's sayings are:

> God has no mercy on one who has no mercy for others.

> None of you truly believes until he wishes for his brother what he wishes for himself.

> Powerful is not he who knocks the other down, indeed the powerful is he who controls himself in a fit of anger.

PRACTICE PEACE
Learn more about Islam

THE HEART OF THE MATTER:
the mission of City Hearts

City Hearts
Kids Say "Yes" to the Arts

"City Hearts: Kids Say 'Yes' To The Arts" is committed to intervene in a loving, supportive and nurturing way to break the cycle of poverty, neglect, abuse, homelessness, delinquency and violence that destroys the lives of our children. Through the discipline and healing of classes, workshops and performing experiences in the arts, City Hearts provides positive role models, enrichment and inspiration for our children to learn to be productive, creative, law-abiding members of society. City Hearts is a non-profit organization that has offered free visual and performing arts classes to children in Los Angeles for over 22 years. Established in 1984 by criminal defense attorneys, Sherry and Bob Jason, City Hearts was founded on the belief that the arts are the most powerful tools to communicate with and rehabilitate troubled youth at risk from gangs and drugs. City Hearts is an integral part of the preventive and rehabilitative effort in Los Angeles, inner city, and serves as a model for youth diversion programs across the country.

PROCEEDS FROM THE SALE OF EACH BOOK GO TO CITY HEARTS

www.CityHearts.org

EARTH RIGHTS INSTITUTE:
   the mission of Earth Rights

EARTH RIGHTS INSTITUTE is dedicated to securing a culture of peace and justice by establishing dynamic worldwide networks of persons of goodwill and special skill, promoting policies and programs which further democratic rights to common heritage resources, and building ecological communities. Earth Rights was started by Annie Goeke and Alanna Hartzok, two women noted for their combined 30 years of community based work focused on successfully affecting our economic, social and environmental challenges in a just and humane way.

PROCEEDS FROM THE SALE OF EACH BOOK GO TO EARTH RIGHTS INSTITUTE

www.EARTHRIGHTS.net

Acknowledgments:

To my husband, **Hubert de La Bouillerie**. Where do I begin? There are simply not enough words to describe my gratitude for all you have given me. Gratitude for your extraordinary vision and creativity, your bold brilliance and indomitable spirit, inexhaustible loving and passionate support of my creative self-expression, fearless nature and total *joie de vivre*. I can't imagine life without you.

To my endorsers: **Deepak Chopra, Gore Vidal, Jane Seymour, Arianna Huffington, Penny Marshall, Debbie Ford, Penney Finkelman Cox, Nicholas Lore, Lois Sarkisian, Daphne Rose Kingma, Les Edgerton, Debra** and **Rachel Marcus, Wendy Newman**...thank you.

To **John-Roger**, my dearest friend and spiritual guide: Thank you for your love and encouragement to write this book. Traveling the realms of consciousness with you has been my greatest joy and privilege.

To **John Morton**: Thank you for living a life that exemplifies a commitment to peace. You light up the way.

To **Uncle Charlie**, aka "Lucky": Your belief in me made much of this possible. I hope you know that. Skybaby dances with joy that our love continues to blossom.

To my bestest friend **Dey**, always my champion: Don't ever stop.

To **Heide Banks**: You always push me beyond my comfort zone. Thank God.

To **Agapi Stassinopoulos**: You are your Greek name — love. Your unending generosity of spirit is a blessing in my life. Thank you for being the incredible "you."

To **Anna Getty** and the **Nimble Jedi's**, support team extraordinaire: Thank you for the gift of your love and Anna, God bless you for my title.

To **Drs. Ron** and **Mary Hulnick** and the **University of Santa Monica** - Class of 2003: It all started with you.

To my brilliant illustrator and friend, **Victor Robert**: You injected my words with visual magic. You are a shining star.

To **Robby Djendrono**, gifted graphic designer and collaborator: I can not thank you enough for your amazing contributions. Anyone who gets to work with you is better for it.

To my entrepreneurial partner and publisher, **Drew Nederpelt**, and to my talented and vigilant Cambridge House editor, **Rachel Trusheim**. You are a winning team. I'm excited we're on this adventure together.

To my great editors: **Pamela Lane**, **Danielle Dorman** and the sage **Lee Cohen**. You raised the bar.

To **Lisa Elia**: You put wind in my sails and I owe you for it. I look forward to a partnership that grows and flourishes over time.

To **Chef Akasha** for all your love and support and telling me I had to work with Lisa Elia.

To **Danielle** and **Ernie Del**: Your generosity of spirit leaves me speechless. Merci beaucoup.

To **Sherry** and **Bob Jason**, **Jane Donaldson** and **the board of City Hearts**: I can't imagine a world without art. You provide that experience to souls on this planet who might get left behind. Bravo! Bravo!

To **Annie Goeke-de La Bouillerie** and **Earth Rights Institute**: Your extraordinary commitment to serve inspires me daily. If we could all connect to the "Annie" inside of us, then peace and justice in this world would become sustainable at last.

To my dearest friends who wrapped their loving arms around me and helped me in any way they could: **Susan Vash and Franck Labbe**, **Kristen** and **George Minardos**, **Jan Eliasberg**, **Mitch Newman**, **Nana Greenwald**, **Lisa Lieberman-Doctor**, **Mitra Lore**, **Rosemond Hammond**, aka The Wild Rose, **Jeff Sklar**, **Daniel** and **Natalie Pitlik**, **Judi Goldfader**, **David Samson**, **Elinor Pruder**, "ma belle mere," **Patti Rayner**, **Leigh Taylor Young**, **Margrit Polak**, **Michael Westphall**, **Dean Erickson**, **David Ladd** and **Harvey Shields**.

And finally to my mother and father, **Sylvia** and **Sy Robins**, who told me I could do anything, including write.

Victor Robert

Victor Robert is both a traditional illustrator and digital 3D computer animator. At the Art Center College of Design, Victor directed a 3D animated short entitled "The Yellow Umbrella," which showed internationally and won a Student Academy Award.

Victor has since established himself in the Hollywood film industry and the advertising world as a unique illustrator, storyteller and visual consultant. His professional portfolio is wide-ranging and includes storyboarding, concept design, and commercial directing for companies such as Mattel, Bombay Sapphire Gin, Klasky Csupo, and Burger King. His film work includes *South Park: Bigger, Longer, and Uncut* and most recently he served as Rough Layout Supervisor for the Paramount Pictures release of *Barnyard the Movie.*

Victor has paired with author Debbie Robins as the illustrator on her upcoming series of books, the next of which is *Where Happiness Lives.* He was born in Puerto Rico and currently lives in the Los Angeles area.

www.victorrobert.com

EXERCISE TO STRENGTHEN YOUR PEACE MUSCLE:

Is there a person you're angry with? Someone whose actions you don't approve of? (write down his or her name)

_____

Please describe what you think is "wrong" about that person. What should he or she do differently? What would make things "right" in your experience?

_____

_____

_____

_____

_____

_____

_____

_____

_____

_____

_____

_____

_____

_____

_____

_____

Consider going to that place of peace inside you. To help you get there you might think of a person you love, a baby, an animal, nature, your God or spiritual teacher. You might choose to place your hand over your heart.

From that place of loving, can you see another way you can look at this person that gives you more peace?

Peace Key # 1:   Can you accept your differences?
Peace Key # 2:   Can you love the person anyway?
Peace Key # 3:   Can you forgive what this person
                   has done, imagining that, if you
                   knew more of the person's story,
                   you'd understand his or her actions?

How do you feel about that person now?

_____

_____

_____

_____

_____

_____

_____

_____

Practice The Three Keys To Peace
You can make a difference

Your Peace Journey

_____
_____
_____
_____
_____
_____
_____
_____
_____
_____
_____
_____
_____
_____
_____
_____
_____
_____
_____
_____
_____

Your Peace Journey

_____

_____

_____

_____

_____

_____

_____

_____

_____

_____

_____

_____

_____

_____

_____

_____

_____

_____

_____

_____

_____

_____

_____

_____

Your Peace Journey

_____

_____

_____

_____

_____

_____

_____

_____

_____

_____

_____

_____

_____

_____

_____

_____

_____

_____

_____

_____

_____

_____

_____

_____

Your Peace Journey

Your Peace Journey

_____

_____

_____

_____

_____

_____

_____

_____

_____

_____

_____

_____

_____

_____

_____

_____

_____

_____

_____

_____

_____

_____

_____

_____

Your Peace Journey

Your Peace Journey

_____
_____
_____
_____
_____
_____
_____
_____
_____
_____
_____
_____
_____
_____
_____
_____
_____
_____
_____
_____
_____
_____
_____

YOUR PEACE JOURNEY

YOUR PEACE JOURNEY

_____

_____

_____

_____

_____

_____

_____

_____

_____

_____

_____

_____

_____

_____

_____

_____

_____

_____

_____

_____

_____

YOUR PEACE JOURNEY

_____

_____

_____

_____

_____

_____

_____

_____

_____

_____

_____

_____

_____

_____

_____

_____

_____

_____

_____

_____

_____

_____

YOUR PEACE JOURNEY

YOUR PEACE JOURNEY

_____

_____

_____

_____

_____

_____

_____

_____

_____

_____

_____

_____

_____

_____

_____

_____

_____

_____

_____

_____

_____

_____

_____

Your Peace Journey

_____

_____

_____

_____

_____

_____

_____

_____

_____

_____

_____

_____

_____

_____

_____

_____

_____

_____

_____

_____

_____

_____

Your Peace Journey

Your Peace Journey

_____
_____
_____
_____
_____
_____
_____
_____
_____
_____
_____
_____
_____
_____
_____
_____
_____
_____
_____
_____
_____
_____
_____
_____
_____